Dear mouse friends,
Welcome to the world of

Geronimo Stilton

THE RODENT'S GAZETTE
EDITORIAL STAFF

Geronimo Stilton
A learned and brainy
mouse; editor of
The Rodent's Gazette

Thea Stilton
Geronimo's sister and
special correspondent at
The Rodent's Gazette

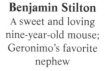

Trap Stilton
An awful joker;
Geronimo's cousin and
owner of the store
Cheap Junk for Less

Benjamin Stilton
A sweet and loving
nine-year-old mouse;
Geronimo's favorite
nephew

Geronimo Stilton

THE PECULIAR PUMPKIN THIEF

Scholastic Inc.

New York   Toronto   London   Auckland

Sydney   Mexico City   New Delhi   Hong Kong

ISBN 978-0-545-10372-5

Copyright © 2003 by Edizioni Piemme S.p.A., via Tiziano 32, 20145 Milan, Italy.

International Rights © Atlantyca S.p.A.

English translation © 2010 by Atlantyca S.p.A.

Based on an idea by Elisabetta Dami.

www.geronimostilton.com

Published by Scholastic Inc., 557 Broadway, New York, NY 10012. SCHOLASTIC and associated logos are trademarks and/or registered trademarks of Scholastic Inc.

Stilton is the name of a famous English cheese. It is a registered trademark of the Stilton Cheese Makers' Association. For more information, go to www.stiltoncheese.com.

Text by Geronimo Stilton
Original title *Lo strano caso della Torre Pagliaccia*
Cover by Lorenzo Chiavini
Illustrations by Lorenzo Chiavini
Graphics by Topea Sha Sha

Special thanks to Kathryn Cristaldi
Special thanks to Lidia Morson Tramontozzi
Interior design by Kay Petronio

12 11 10 9 8 7 6 5 4 3 2 1   10 11 12 13 14 15/0

Printed in the U.S.A.   40
First printing, July 2010

THE GREATEST HALLOWEEN PARTY EVER!

It was a cold, rainy October night. On the streets of New Mouse City, the **HOWLING WIND** threatened to rip my favorite CHEESE-COLORED umbrella right out of my paws!

Rat's whiskers! How I wished I were home relaxing in my comfy cat-fur slippers.

Instead I was heading downtown to . . .

OOPS! I did it again! When will I ever remember to introduce myself? My

name is Stilton, *Geronimo Stilton*. I am the publisher of *The Rodent's Gazette*, the most famouse newspaper on Mouse Island.

Anyway, where was I? Oh, yes, I was heading downtown to meet *my favorite nephew*, Benjamin. It was only a few days until HALLOWEEN, and I had promised him I would throw a Halloween party at my house. We would invite all of his friends.

"Ready to go shopping for the party?" I asked the little mouse.

Benjamin's **smile** made me forget all about the dreary weather.

"This is going to be the **GREATEST** Halloween party ever!" he squeaked. "You're the **best**, Uncle Geronimo!"

Did I mention I have the **sweetest** nephew on the planet?

Yoo-Hoo!

I took Benjamin to **TRICKS FOR TAILS**, the most popular party store in New Mouse City. It has lots of decorations, weird gadgets, and party pranks.

When we entered the store, we were greeted by the owner, **Paws Prankster**. One thing you should know about **Paws**: He loves to test out his pranks on unsuspecting customers.

Of course, today was no exception.

"Like my ring?" he giggled, waving his paw in my face.

I took a closer look, and a stream of water squirted me in the snout!

Cheese niblets!

"Got ya!" **Paws** guffawed.

"Look at this, Uncle," Benjamin said, pointing to a **humongous** orange pumpkin.

I had to admit it was pretty impressive.

But why had someone left a banana peel on top of the pumpkin? How strange!

Benjamin found a rack with lots of scary costumes.

He tried on a GHOST, an ALIEN, and a SKELETON costume.

They were all so **SPOOKY**, we couldn't decide. We decided to think it over and come back in a few days.

We were about to leave when I felt someone — or something — tug on my tail.

I turned around, but there was no one there. How odd!

I took another step. Again I felt a tug on my tail.

AT TRICKS FOR TAILS:

1. Disgusting green slime
2. Plastic Swiss cheese with punching glove
3. Fluorescent fur dye
4. Giant bat with glow-in-the-dark eyes
5. Ghost costume
6. Bogeyman
7. Rubber snake
8. Jack-o'-lantern
9. Stink bombs
10. Hairy spiders
11. Plastic skull
12. Spider magnet
13. Squirt ring

I whirled around fast, but still no one was there. **How weird!**

A rubber bat dangling from the ceiling stared at me with evil eyes. **YIKES!** I was beginning to get the creeps.

At that moment, the giant pumpkin began to move.

"Yoo-hoo!" a voice whispered.

Suddenly, a furry gray snout popped out of the pumpkin.

Yoo-hoo!

Hercule?

"Like my little joke, Stilton?" the mouse giggled.

I should have known. It was my friend **Hercule Poirat**, the famouse detective. Hercule loves to play pranks, and he's always eating bananas.

"Stilton, I could really use your help solving a HALLOWEEN **MYSTERY**...." he began.

But I cut him off.

Hercule loved to get me to help with his crazy cases, but I wasn't about to get involved. I had a HALLOWEEN party to plan!

"Sorry, Hercule, no time," I said quickly.

Then I took Bejamin by the paw and **RAN** out the door before **Hercule** could stop me.

IF YOU'VE SEEN
THESE PUMPKINS . . .

The next day, I went back to **TRICKS FOR TAILS**. I was going to buy the giant jack-o'-lantern and a few other scary decorations to surprise Benjamin.

But when I got there, there was nothing left: no **TRICKS**, no DECORATIONS, no costumes.

"I was robbed!" **PAWS PRANKSTER** sobbed. "They took everything!"

I looked around. This time, **PAWS** wasn't pulling my paw. The **robbers** had taken *everything*.

Right then, the phone rang.

PAWS blew his nose — **HONK!** — then answered the phone. He chatted for a

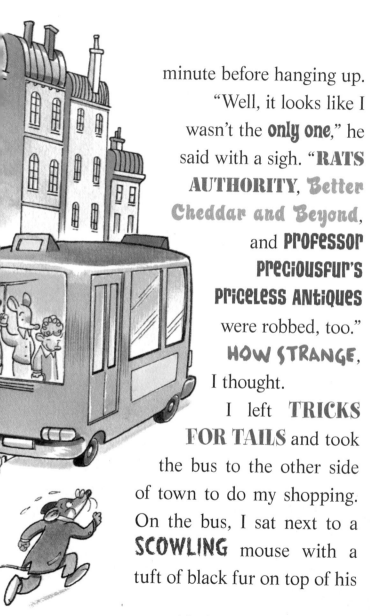

minute before hanging up. "Well, it looks like I wasn't the **only one**," he said with a sigh. "**RATS AUTHORITY, Better Cheddar and Beyond,** and **PROFESSOR PRECIOUSFUR'S PRICELESS ANTIQUES** were robbed, too." **HOW STRANGE,** I thought.

I left **TRICKS FOR TAILS** and took the bus to the other side of town to do my shopping. On the bus, I sat next to a **SCOWLING** mouse with a tuft of black fur on top of his head and three silver rings in his snout. He was chattering into his cell phone.

"Can you believe it?" I heard him squeak. "Last night, some rat robbed the 🅿🆁🅰🅽🅺 🅵🅰🅲🆃🅾🆁🆈. Now where am I supposed to get a scary costume for Squeaky's Halloween party?"

I was about to tell Snout Rings he already looked pretty scary to me when we reached my stop.

I jumped off the bus and headed for the farmers' market. I knew I could find a HALLOWEEN pumpkin there. But I was in for another surprise. All of the pumpkins had been stolen!

Instead, I saw a TV crew interviewing a farmer. He was holding up pictures of his MISSING PRODUCE.

"If you've seen these pumpkins," he squeaked, "please call the **POLICE**."

I started thinking. First **TRICKS FOR TAILS**. Then the P R A N K F A C T O R Y. THEN ALL OF THE PUMPKINS iN NEW MOUSE CiTY!

It looked like someone was out to sabotage HALLOWEEN.

But Who? Who?

PRANK FACTORY

Who?

Whooooooo?

GLOPPY
GREEN SLIME

There was only one thing to do. I ran to the office of **Hercule Poirat**. As I said, Hercule is a great detective. Unfortunately, his office is less than great. In fact, it's a **DISASTER**.

I knocked on the door to his flea-infested shack. **Cheese niblets**, the place was a **DUMP**!

I was about to pull out my paw sanitizer when I heard a clanking sound.

I looked up and a bucket filled with **worms** and gloppy **green slime** poured down on me.

"**HEEEEEEEEEEEEEELP!**" I squeaked.

The door flew open and **Hercule Poirat** peeked out.

"Is that you, Stilton? How do you like my new **ANTi-SPy** trap?" he asked, grinning.

I pulled the bucket off my head.

Oh, how did I get myself into these messes? I'm *Geronimo Stilton*. I'm a good mouse. I wear a helmet when I ride my bike. I cross on the **green**, not in between. I never litter. Well, except for that one time the wind whipped a **Cheesy Chew** wrapper out of my paws when I was driving on the freeway.

"**What brings you here, Geronimo?**" Hercule asked, interrupting my thoughts.

"I'm ready to help you solve this HALLOWEEN mystery," I declared.

Hercule picked up a suitcase near the door. He told me he was off to check out some SUSPICIOUS activity.

"I'll call you
when I know more!"
he squeaked.
"**Hercule**, wait!"
I called.
But he was
already *gone*.

OPEN . . .
IF YOU DARE!

The morning before Halloween, I woke up **early**. I had a lot to do to prepare for my Halloween party. I was sweeping my stoop when I noticed a bright orange-colored envelope in my mailbox. On it was written: **"Open . . . if you dare!"**

Inside was a sheet with a strange poem:

You're invited to my
Halloween party,

Please do your best
not to be tardy.

I've planned a great night
full of games and prizes,

And all the best music,
rides, and surprises.

Candy corn, caramel apples, and,
of course, lots of cheese,

The food is all free —
eat as much as you please!

You don't know my name, but
we'll meet tomorrow night:

Come to Mystery Park when the
moon's shining bright.

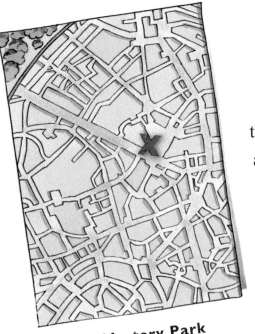

X: Mystery Park

On the back of the invitation was a map on how to get to Mystery Park. It was all very **STRANGE**. I mean, I'd never even heard of a place called **Mystery Park**.

I decided to make some **hot cheddar**. Sometimes I think more clearly with a **steamy** mug of **hot cheddar** in my paws. I was still trying to make sense of the invitation when my doorbell rang.

It was my cousin Trap, my sister, Thea, and my nephew Benjamin. Each of them was waving an **ORANGE** envelope.

"Hey, Gerry Berry, I see you got the invite,

too!" my cousin squeaked. "Fabarooni! We can all go together!"

I chewed my whiskers.

"Not so fast, Trap," I warned. "How do we even know who sent this? I don't like accepting invitations from STRANGERS."

Trap guffawed.

"Oh, don't get your fur in a frenzy, Geronimoid. Everybody's going. Plus, someone stole all the HALLOWEEN stuff in town. How else are you going to celebrate?" my cousin demanded.

A FACE LIKE A ZOMBIE

Then he added, "And, you don't even need a costume, Cousinkins. You've already got a face like a Zombie."

I ignored him.

"Why don't you all come to **my house** instead?" I asked. "We don't need **DECORATIONS** to have fun on HALLOWEEN."

Trap smirked. Thea rolled her eyes. And Benjamin's shoulders **SLUMPED**. "Are you sure you don't want to go to the party, Uncle Geronimo?" he asked.

I gave in.

How could I say no to my favorite nephew?

WHAT IS IT?

That night, I couldn't get to sleep. Just when I'd drift off, I'd be woken up by what sounded like someone revving up their car engine right outside my window. How rude!

The next morning, I stumbled out of bed. I was determined to find the late-night noisemaker and give him a piece of my mind. But when I got outside, I couldn't believe my eyes. Smack in the middle of town, a gigantic tower seemed to have risen right out of the ground. It was covered by an orange tarp.

A crowd stood GAPING at the tower with open snouts.

"What is it?" asked

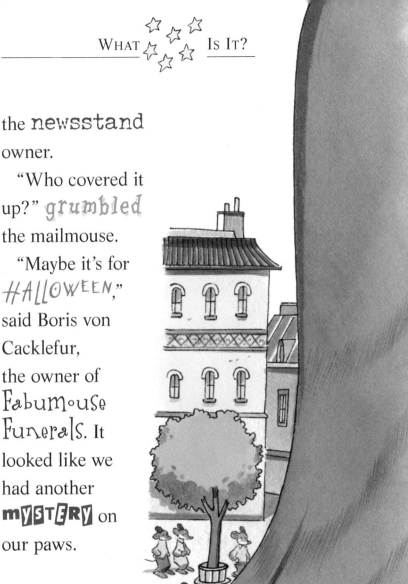

the newsstand owner.

"Who covered it up?" grumbled the mailmouse.

"Maybe it's for HALLOWEEN," said Boris von Cacklefur, the owner of Fabumouse Funerals. It looked like we had another MYSTERY on our paws.

A CREEPY KIND OF MUSIC

Halloween had finally arrived. What a strange day. All afternoon, a creepy, eerie kind of music could be heard throughout town.

Come to Mystery Park
As soon as it's dark.
You'll shiver with fright
And munch treats all night!
So come if you dare—
I'll meet you all there!

As soon as the sun went down, my family showed up on my doorstep. "Get your tail in gear, Germeister," my cousin announced. "We're off to Mystery Park."

Reluctantly, I followed them outside. I was still feeling nervous about the mysterious invitation. I couldn't put my paw on it, but something just didn't seem right.

As we headed for the park, I noticed a ton of rodents all going in the same direction. It seemed like the entire city would be celebrating HALLOWEEN at Mystery Park!

"This is going to be fabumouse," I heard one rodent remark.

"I can't wait to try the cheese treats," another added.

"And it's all FREE!" a third squeaked.

Everyone was so excited. I tried to shake off my nerves. After all, it was a party. What was there to be nervous about? It was just a DARK Halloween night, and I was going to a party thrown by someone I'd never met. I gulped. Oh, why was I always such a SCAREDY mouse?

Just as I was about to enter the park, my cell phone rang.

I looked at the number. It was **Hercule Poirat**.

There was a lot of **static** on the phone.

"DON'T . . . O . . . ARK . . . DAN . . . ROOOOOOUS!" he squeaked.

"What did you say? I can't hear you!" I shouted.

But it was **TOO LATE**. The call had been disconnected.

A minute later, I was pushed along by the crowd into **Mystery Park**.

The heavy gates slammed shut behind me.

IT'S JUST A PARTY

I started to panic. Why was I feeling so trapped? *Get a grip, Geronimo,* I told myself. *It's just a party.* And what an amazing party it was!

There was music and rides and food galore. Plus, everyone entering the park was given a clown mask. Sort of like a door prize, I guess. Rodents dressed in clown costumes passed out all kinds of yummy treats.

I tried to *relax*, but I still felt uneasy. Who

Cotton candy!

Peanuts!

Candy!

EVERYTHING IS FREE!

Cheese pastries!

Cupcakes!

would throw an extravagant HALLOWEEN party and invite a whole city of strangers? And what was up with the clown costumes?

I was trying to figure it out when someone clapped me on the back.

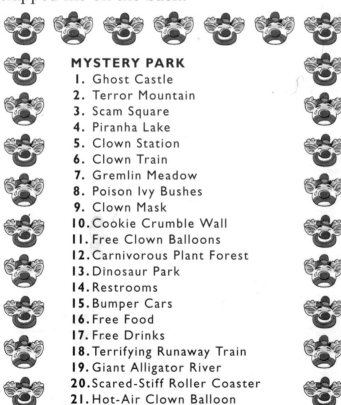

MYSTERY PARK
1. Ghost Castle
2. Terror Mountain
3. Scam Square
4. Piranha Lake
5. Clown Station
6. Clown Train
7. Gremlin Meadow
8. Poison Ivy Bushes
9. Clown Mask
10. Cookie Crumble Wall
11. Free Clown Balloons
12. Carnivorous Plant Forest
13. Dinosaur Park
14. Restrooms
15. Bumper Cars
16. Free Food
17. Free Drinks
18. Terrifying Runaway Train
19. Giant Alligator River
20. Scared-Stiff Roller Coaster
21. Hot-Air Clown Balloon

HAVE FUN!

I nearly **JUMPED** out of my fur.

"Hey, JUMPY GERRY! What's the matter?" my cousin Trap asked as he smirked. Then he waved a **TRIPLE-DECKER** cheese sandwich in my snout. "Is this free food **scaring** you?"

Next to him, Benjamin was **happily** munching on **cheddar popcorn**.

"**Taste some**, Uncle Geronimo," he offered.

Mayor Frederick Fuzzypaws

William Shortpaws

The Postmaster

Tina Spicytail

Professor Paws von Volt

Thea sipped a **megasize** milk shake. "**LOOSEN UP**, Gerrykins," Thea said. "You look like you're in the dentist's chair about to have a **ROOT CANAL**."

I looked around and saw all my friends.

Everyone was having such a *wonderful* time.

Everyone, that is, except **ME**. Oh, why did I have such a bad feeling?

...cle Samuel S. Stingysnout

Sally Ratmousen

Boris von Cacklefur

Creepella von Cacklefur

Nancy Neatfur

Pinky Pick

Nibblette

I WANT
MY MOMMY!

Suddenly, all the lights **WENT OUT** in
the park.

Holey cheese! What was happening? I
heard a rustling sound nearby. In the **darkness**,
I could make out a pack of rodents dressed in
clown costumes. They scurried through the
FRONT GATE, locking it behind them.

Then a **SCARY** voice rang out:

"Welcome, strangers, to Mystery Park.
I'm so glad that you fell for my trap in the dark.
That's right — my assistants have locked all the gates.
So forget about leaving — just sit down and wait.
Yes, while you were laughing and talking and eating,
I surrounded your houses for my own trick-or-treating.
So sit tight, foolish mice, I'll be done soon enough.
I'm the best of the best at stealing your stuff!"

I gulped. What a NIGHTMARE! All of the rodents around me began to scamper around. Some tugged at the iron gates, but they were impossible to open. They were all bolted with enormouse LOCKS.

Others tried to climb the walls. But these were no ordinary walls. They were covered with creamy **whipped chocolate**! It was perfect for eating, but not so great for climbing. Mice were SLiPPiNG AND SLiDiNG all over the place.

"I want OUT of here!" a rodent fumed.

"I want my LAWYER!" another one squeaked.

"I want my mommy!" I sobbed hysterically.

Oh, I knew I should have stayed in my cozy mouse hole!

Do You Know How to Fly a Helicopter?

At that moment, I heard the **thunderous** roar of a helicopter.

I looked up. A helicopter with a clown face was flying above us. In the light of the moon, I could just make out the pilot. He wore a trench coat and was waving a banana in the air.

I cleaned my glasses, then I looked again. Yes, it was **Hercule Poirat**! Who else would fly a **HELICOPTER** and eat a banana at the same time?

"Stilton, grab hold of the hook!" he yelled.

I looked around. Hook? What was Hercule talking about? A minute later, a huge steel

hook dropped from the helicopter and bonked me on the head. **Youch!** I squeezed my eyes shut tight, grabbed it, and hung on for **dear life**.

I yelled down to Thea, Trap, and Benjamin. "Don't **worry**! I'll be back soon to get everyone out!"

With a **jerk**, I was reeled up into the plane. Hercule shoved a headset onto my head so we could communicate with each other over the **ROAR** of the engine.

Soon we were flying high over the park. The wind was like a cyclone **WHIPPING** my whiskers all over the place. I made a mental note to remember to book an appointment with **Clip Rat**, my barber. It would

take weeks to **UNTANGLE** this fur!

Just then, the helicopter took a **nosedive**, and I let out an ear-piercing squeak.

"Um, Hercule. D-d-d-o you know h-h-h-how to fly a helicopter?" I stammered.

I stole a quick glance at my friend. He had a funny smile on his face.

"Don't be silly, Stilton. I've definitely flown a helicopter before." He grinned. "Maybe not a **REAL** one, but I had loads of 🄣🄞🄨 airplanes when I was young."

MOLDY MOZZARELLA! I was a passenger in a helicopter flown by a mouse whose only experience as a pilot was playing with tiny plastic planes! I began to feel FAINT. Tiny dots of light swam in front of my eyes. Well, maybe that was because it was nighttime and we were hurtling past lots of **STARS**. But you get the point. I was a bundle of **nerves**!

"We've got to **RESCUE** our friends!" I shrieked at Hercule. But he shook his head. "First we need to find 𝒞𝒽𝓊𝒸𝓀𝓁𝑒𝓈!" he said.

𝒞𝒽𝓊𝒸𝓀𝓁𝑒𝓈? Who was my friend talking about? Maybe the altitude was affecting his brain cells. I was about to suggest we head for the nearest hospital when Hercule began to explain.

It seemed a *thiEF* who called himself 𝒞𝒽𝓊𝒸𝓀𝓁𝑒𝓈 had decided to rip off New Mouse City. First he stole all the HALLOWEEN supplies in town, then he built Mystery Park and invited

everybody to a party. After everyone had gathered, he **LOCKED** the gates and began LOOTING all the houses.

"He's got an army of mice helping him, and they're all dressed like clowns!" Hercule finished.

I was *stunned*. So that was what my friend had called to warn me about. Too bad I hadn't been able to hear him.

"Oh, and one more thing," Hercule added. "This helicopter? It's Chuckles's private helicopter. Can you imagine how **MAD** he's going to be when he finds out I STOLE it?"

At that moment, I heard a sound more **HORRIFYING** than a hissing cat. More **PETRIFYING** than pawnails on a chalkboard. It was the **roar** of helicopters — smaller clown helicopters. *And they were headed right for us!*

I REALLY DESERVE A LITTLE SNACK!

"We're being followed!" I shrieked in a panic as the clown copters grew closer.

But **Hercule** just laughed. That mouse loves a challenge. With a gleeful **squeak**, he yanked on the control stick, then began doing **somersaults** in midair.

A wave of nausea hit me. I grabbed an airsickness bag.

"Weak stomach, Geronimo?" Hercule smirked.

I couldn't answer. I was turning as **GREEN** as a stalk of celery.

Did I mention that I get airsick? And carsick. And seasick.

GLBBBBBBBBBB!

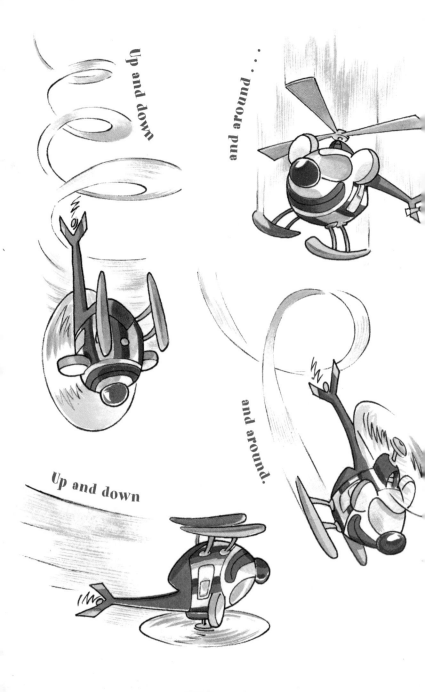

Oh, and I also get sick when I watch clothes *tumbling* around in the dryer at the Squeaky Clean Laundromat. But that's another story.

Even though my stomach was hurting, I still noticed the **STRANGE** activity going on in the streets far below. Clowns were everywhere. They were rANsAⒸKiⓃG the city! Houses, stores, banks. The clowns were stealing everything!

Luckily, **Hercule** was able to lose the clown helicopters that were chasing us.

"**Another job well done!**" he congratulated himself. Then he pulled a banana out of his coat pocket.

"I **really** deserve a little snack," he announced as he *SHOVED* the fruit in his mouth and flipped the peel over his shoulder.

But the peel got **STUCK** under the control panel.

"**Oops**," Hercule muttered.

Two minutes later, the helicopter began sputtering in the air.

I looked out the window and saw the sea under us.

The **WAVES** were getting nearer and nearer and nearer!

SPLASHHH!

Before I could scream, we hit the water. The helicopter began to **SiNK**.

glub glub glub glub glub glub glub glub glub

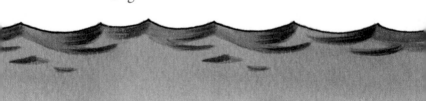

WE WERE DOOMED!

I watched in horror as the helicopter began to fill up with water. **Hercule** was passed out by my side.

We were **doomed**! I saw my life **FLASH** before my eyes — my first step, my first squeak, my first **chocolate Cheesy Chew**. Yum. I love **Cheesy Chews**. I promised myself if I made it out of this alive I'd treat myself to one whole box. Or maybe two.

But there was no time to think about **Cheesy Chews** now. I had to think **FAST**. I knew that the external water

pressure would prevent me from opening the helicopter door. So I waited until the entire helicopter filled up with waterR. Then I grabbed Hercule by the tail and pushed open the door.

The water was ICY.

And it was so DARK at the bottom of the sea.

Above me, the light from the moon made the waves SHIMMER. I swam desperately toward the surface. My lungs were about to EXPLODE. But I had to keep going. For my friend, for my family, and, okay, I admit it — for those delicious chocolate Cheesy Chews!

Finally, I reached the surface. "I did it!" I squeaked.

FISH FOOD!

Right then, **Hercule** came to. "What happened? What are we doing in the water? What's for dinner?" he babbled.

Before I could respond, I noticed lights on shore. The clowns were looking for us! We hid under a pier. Too bad there was a sewer nearby. The stench was unbelievable.

Footsteps thundered above us.

Two clowns stood on the pier. Their evil laughs filled the **dark** night.

"That copter sank like a **BRICK**!" we heard one say.

"Those rodents are **fish food** now!" another giggled.

"Let's tell the boss. He's at the Clown Tower.

He just got rid of the tarp that was on top of the building."

Hercule nudged me.

So that's what the **Mysterious** cloth-covered skyscraper was all about: It was the **thief's headquarters**!

THE CLOWN TOWER

As soon as the clowns left, we splashed out of the water. It felt good to be on dry land. But what was that **AWFUL SMELL**? I **sniffed** the air. Then it hit me. The **stench** was coming from my own fur! Putrid cheese puffs! I smelled just like a **SEWER RAT**!

Putrid cheese puffs!

AN ARMY OF CLOWNS

I was dying to wash off my fur in a nice relaxing **bubble bath**, but there was no time to waste. We had work to do. We had to find Chuckles before he left town with all our stuff.

Just then, I remembered the clown masks we had been given at Mystery Park. I had one for me and one for Benjamin. Now I pulled both masks from my pocket.

"Let's put on these clown masks so **no one** will notice us," I told Hercule.

We headed toward the center of the city. When we arrived, I choked back tears. What a dreadful sight! An army of clowns marched through the streets stealing everything —

jewelry, television sets, video equipment, computers, food, and clothing. They dragged **HUGE** sacks of **MONEY** from the New Mouse City Bank. They emptied everything into clown cars.

With a heavy heart, I watched as the thieves carried **priceless** artwork out of the National Mouseum. They even **stole** the *Mona Mousa*!

Then they marched up the stairs to The Rodent's Gazette.

I couldn't watch anymore.

"What kind of a **MADMOUSE** would want to ransack a *whole city*?" I whispered to **Hercule**.

MONA MOUSA

As we headed toward the tower, Hercule gave me the lowdown on *Chuckles*.

Chuckles

Who is he: An evil clown.

What does he do: Commands an army of evil clowns to rob Mouse Island.

His dream: To become hilariously rich.

Unusual features: He lives in an extremely tall tower shaped like a clown.

His obsession: He collects clown shoes.

His secret: He loves to knit.

His strong point: He is very funny and can fool anyone — even his own grandmother.

His weak point: He is very sentimental and sobs like a newborn at sad stories.

WHAT ARE YOU WAITING FOR?

At last, we reached the Clown Tower. I saw a line of clown cars coming and going. The clowns were piling up the **stolen goods** and heading back for more.

Hmmm. How would we get close to the **TOWER** without being noticed?

"What we need is another plane," **Hercule** suggested. "No one can grab us while we're in the air."

Just then, I saw a three-wheeled contraption attached to a huge **clown-faced** kite.

"It's a motorized hang glider!" Hercule **squealed**. "And look, those two **FOOLS** are guarding it!"

What luck!

Quietly, we Scampered over to the plane. The two guards were playing **ring-around-the-rosy** with each other.

When they finished, they collapsed.

"That was fun," said one of the guards. "But now I'm tired."

"Guess the boss won't mind if we take a **little snooze**," said the other guard.

A minute later, the two guards were **snoring** like babies.

Hercule sprang into action. He raced over to the hang glider and turned on the motor.

"What are you waiting for, Geronimo?" he squeaked excitedly. "Climb on!"

Suddenly, I realized what I was about to do. My paws began to shake **UNCONTROLLABLY**.

"Um, **Hercule**, do you know how to **FLY** this thing?" I asked.

Hercule grinned gleefully. "Don't be **SILLY**, Geronimo. Of course I know how to fly a glider," he said. Then he added, "Maybe not a **real** one, but I flew loads of paper gliders when I was a **little mouseling**."

My fur turned **pale**.

"We're off!" Hercule cried as the glider rose and dipped in the sky like a **SEASICK** pigeon.

Hercule took a banana out of his pocket.

"I deserve a little snack!" he announced.

I gulped. I wondered if it was possible to die from fright.

THE CLOWN TOWER

The hang glider lifted us HiꝽHeR AND HiꝽHeR into the air. I chewed my whiskers to stop myself from screaming.

Then, way down below, we spotted it. An IMMENSE statue of a clown rose from the ground.

The Clown Tower!

A flower on top of the statue's hat spun around at regular intervals. It was a RADAR detector. It looked like Chuckles was serious about keeping away trespassers.

I closed my eyes as Hercule plunked the hang glider down on the edge of the statue. Whew! The radar JUST MiSSeD US!

I stepped gingerly away from the glider,

We're landing!

trying not to look down. Did I mention I'm afraid of **HEIGHTS**? Meanwhile, **Hercule** was busy munching bananas. He threw the peels on the ground. I followed behind him, picking them up. One thing you should know about Hercule: He's the biggest **LiTTeRbug** on the block!

There was a small door in the ear of the statue. We opened it. Did I mention that I really, really **H A T E** small spaces? And

YUM-YUM-YUM-YUM-YUM!

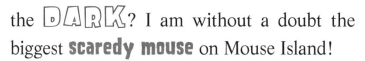

the **DARK**? I am without a doubt the biggest **scaredy mouse** on Mouse Island!

The door led to a lonnnnnnng, dark flight of stairs. It was so **SPOOKY**. I was **SCARED** out of my skull.

WE CREPT DOWN THE STAIRS AS QUIET AS MICE.

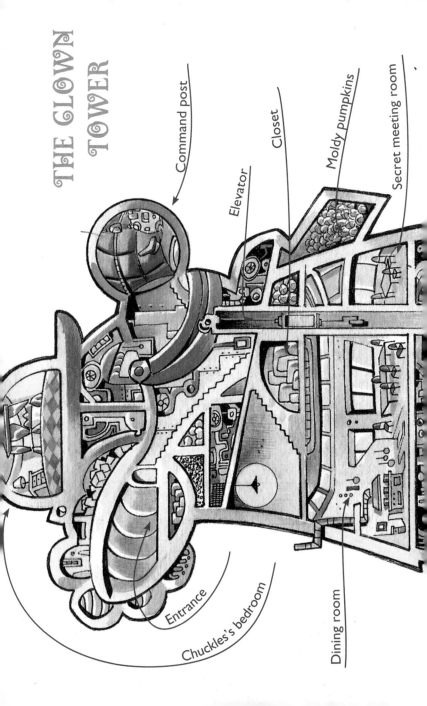

THE CLOWN TOWER

Command post

Elevator

Closet

Moldy pumpkins

Secret meeting room

Entrance

Chuckles's bedroom

Dining room

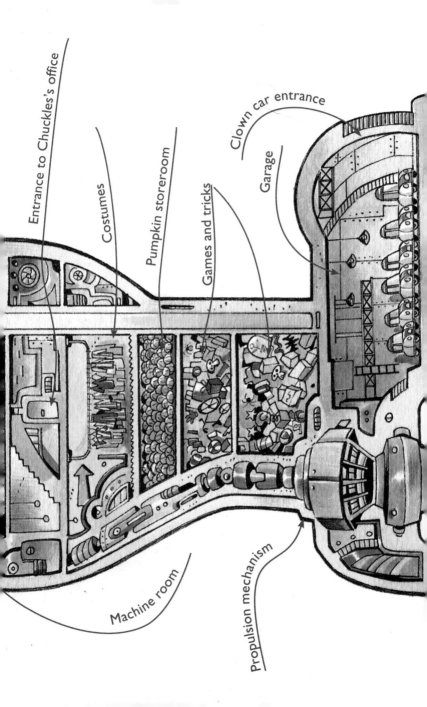

Entrance to Chuckles's office

Costumes

Pumpkin storeroom

Games and tricks

Clown car entrance

Garage

Machine room

Propulsion mechanism

113

113TH FLOOR!

We came to an elevator.

On the wall was a map of the tower with an inscription:

You are on the 113th floor!

I began to feel TRAPPED.

"We have to get . . ." I started to squeak.

But **Hercule** interrupted me.

"Yes, we have to get to Chuckles," he said.

Hercule nudged me into the elevator and the doors slid shut behind me.

He pushed a button that read: 100th floor: Chuckles's office!

I wanted to cry. I wanted to **SCREAM**. I wanted to run to the *Restful Rodent* for a massage with cheese-scented oils.

"We have to get out of here," I whispered. But it was too late.

Ding!

The elevator had arrived on the 100th floor. The doors opened into Chuckles's office.

I KNEW
IT WAS YOU!

Chuckles's office looked just like the inside of a circus tent!

There was a huge stage and lots of brightly colored lights. And in the center of the stage sat . . . Chuckles!

He wore WHITE gloves, a yellow wig, and a little red hat. His blue pants were super baggy, and his yellow tie was dotted with purple polka dots. His black shoes were so oversized I wondered how he managed to walk without falling flat on his face.

We watched as Chuckles picked up something

orange from a big orange pile in the corner. What was *Chuckles* doing?

We crept closer. He was **CARVING** a **pumpkin**!

When he finished, he looked at it with satisfaction.

Then he sang a little song in a high-pitched voice,

"Oh, this Halloween is the best!
 I'll be richer than all of the rest!
 I'll steal all of the money!
 Oh, aren't I funny?
 This Halloween is the best!"

What a rotten, low-down, no-good rat, I fumed to myself. He had stolen from all of the good mice of New Mouse City! Hadn't anyone ever told him that **stealing** is

wrong? Without thinking, I let out a loud **SNORT**.

Uh-oh. The clown heard me and screamed,

"Who's there?

Show your face in my place!"

We approached timidly, our clown masks still on our faces. He looked at us suspiciously and yelled,

"What's with the clothes?

Why are you in those?"

Hercule spoke right up.

"Chief, we took our uniforms to the cleaners," he offered. But **Chuckles** didn't seem to be **BUYING** it. He stared at us skeptically. Then he pointed to me, and boasted,

"You're dressed just like Stilton,
the newpaper mouse.
He thinks he's so smart,
but I'll steal his whole house!"

I groaned inwardly. I pictured the clown army ransacking my house and making off with my precious antique cheese rinds and my Encyclopaedia Ratannica collection.

Then Chuckles pointed his paw in Hercule's face and said with a smirk,

"And you're dressed like Poirat,
the detective, that's who!
He such a big slob,
he belongs in a zoo!"

I could hear Hercule gnashing his teeth. A minute later, he whipped off his mask.

"I'll tell you who belongs in a zoo, **CLOWN FACE**!" Hercule shouted.

Chuckles shrieked, "**I knew it was you!**"

Then he jumped to his feet. It took him a little while because of those **oversized shoes**.

WATCH MY SHOW

I shivered. What would Chuckles do to us now?

Chuckles let out a **cruel laugh**. His nose **lit up** when he was excited. Or maybe he had a sinus infection. It was hard to tell.

He put his paws around us. Then he said, **"I'll let you both go if you watch my show."** His show?

Chuckles challenged us to a contest. He would do his act. And if we did not *laugh*, he would let us go.

That sounded easy. After all, I consider myself an **INTELLECTUAL** mouse with a **sophisticated** sense of humor. Silly clown jokes wouldn't work on me.

We agreed. Chuckles began.

First he jumped
into a little car.
He pressed the
horn, and water
squirted
him in his face.

Next he
pretended to
trip and smacked his snout
on the floor.

Oopsy-daisy!

He turned out the **lights**. Then he pulled a glow-in-the-dark skull out of his hat.

Ha-ha-ha-ha!

He made a thousand *funny* faces.

He sat on a
**whoopee
cushion**.

Prrrrrrrrrrrrt!

Achoo!

He threw a
pepper bomb
that made
us both
sneeze.

Then he threw a **stink** bomb.

And he made a fake spider JUMP from his pocket.

Smack!

Finally, Chuckles took a giant rubber hammer and smacked Hercule in the head. My friend giggled. Then he began to LAUGH.

I couldn't believe it. How could Hercule fall for the old rubber hammer trick? It was so SILLY. It was so RIDICULOUS.

Then Chuckles hit *me* in the head with the hammer. I burst out laughing. I couldn't help it. It was too FUNNY.

"I won!" Chuckles declared.

I won!

POOR STRAWBERRY!

I was **crushed**. I stopped laughing immediately and began to cry.

"**GET A GRIP**, Geronimo!" **Hercule** ordered. "I've got an idea."

He told Chuckles he was challenging him to another contest. "If I can make you cry, then I win," he said.

Chuckles hesitated.

"What's the matter, **Clown Face**? You're not chicken, are you?" Hercule teased.

That did it. The clown rolled his eyes and said, "**I accept your dare. Like I really care.**"

Hercule winked at me. Then he began his story.

"Once upon a time, there was a **teeny tiny**

mouse who lived in a **teeny tiny** house deep in the woods. One day, the **teeny tiny** mouse was out looking for food when he spotted a **HUGE RED STRAWBERRY**. He pushed and he pulled and he dragged the strawberry all the way back to his house. Then he was so tired he took a nap, dreaming of **STRAWBERRY PIE**. But while he was sleeping a big, hungry wolf came by. "Oh, what a delicious-looking combo meal," he said. And so he opened his **GREAT BIG** mouth and gobbled up the strawberry and the **teeny tiny** mouse in one giant **gulp**! The end."

Chuckles's lip began to quiver. Then two big tears slid down his cheeks. Then he rolled on the ground, sobbing uncontrollably and blowing his nose in his **polka-dotted** handkerchief.

Waaah!

"Poor strawberry! Poor mouse!" he cried.

I nodded, wiping tears from my own eyes. What can I say? I'm a sensitive mouse, too.

Meanwhile, Hercule made Chuckles tell us the secret password that opened the locks to Mystery Park.

But just as we were about to leave, Chuckles ran to a small round room filled with levers and switches.

He hit a few buttons. Then the whole room began to RUMBLE!

YOU WILL BE MINE

What was happening?! Was it a **tornado**? Was it an **earthquake**?

Just then, I realized the noise was coming from inside. The whole tower **shook**. Then we rose into the air. Yes, the Clown Tower had turned into a giant **FLYING MACHINE**!

Chuckles began to sing a little song.

"You can't get away from me!

I need some friends, you see.

And you will be mine

Until the end of time—

Yes, you'll keep me company!"

Wow! Chuckles's **CHEESE** really had **SLIPPED** off his cracker.

Next to me, **Hercule** stamped his foot. "We

don't want to go with you!" he shouted. "You can't **FORCE** someone to be your friend!"

Annoyed, 𝒞𝒽𝓊𝒸𝓀𝓁𝑒𝓈 pressed a button. In a flash, two windows on which we were leaning opened.

"**Too bad for you!**" he yelled.

A minute later, we found ourselves **hurtling** into space.

Hmm. Maybe being forced to travel the world with a **CRAZED CLOWN** *wasn't such a bad idea after all*, I thought as my life **FLASHED** before my eyes.

But then I heard something snap. Miraculously, a **YELLOW** parachute opened above us.

"Good thing I listened to **Granny Ironwhiskers** this morning when she reminded me to

Granny
Ironwhiskers
Poirat

take my chute!"
Hercule chuckled.
"Yessirree,
I never
leave home
without it!"

Heeeeelp!

PARTY AT MY HOUSE!

We landed outside the giant **GATES** to **Mystery Park**. I punched in the **password** Chuckles had given us, and the gates swung open.

Our friends swarmed out. Benjamin gave me a **giant hug**. "I knew you'd **SAVE** us, Uncle Geronimo!" he squeaked. "Too bad we didn't get to celebrate HALLOWEEN this year."

I sighed. But then I had an idea. Who says HALLOWEEN can only be one night of the year?

"Let's have a HALLOWEEN party at my house tomorrow night," I told my nephew.

AS MY GRANDMOTHER SAYS . . .

The next day, I worked like a **MADMOUSE** getting things ready for the party. I cleaned my mouse hole from top to bottom. Then I made my own *HALLOWEEN* decorations.

I drew **PICTURES** of pumpkins, GHOSTS, and **BATS** on construction paper. Then I cut them out and hung them up all over my house. I filled a glass pitcher with punch and labeled it VAMPIRE JUICE.

Before I knew it, it was time for my party to begin. I wrapped myself up in **toilet paper**.

Just as I finished, the doorbell rang. Guests streamed into my house. I welcomed a **MONSTER**, an alien, a **ZOMBIE**, and more.

I must admit, some of the costumes were pretty **scary**. I had to keep reminding myself that they were all my friends. Still, my knees shook every time I passed by Frankenstein. And Count Dracula's **FANGS** were positively **FUR-RAISING**!

I was trying to calm my nerves when **Hercule Poirat** showed up. He was dressed in his usual **YELLOW TRENCH COAT** and hat.

"Where's your costume?" I asked.

Hercule **scratched** his head. "This *is* my costume," he said. "I'm dressed like a **DETECTiVE**."

Detective · Alien · Zombie · Witch · Count Drac

Then he added, **"As Granny Ironwhiskers says, always be yourself."**

I snickered. "Um, **Hercule**, I don't think she was talking about *HALLOWEEN* costumes," I said.

Hercule bristled. "Are you making **fun** of my grandmother, Geronimo?" he accused. "I'll have you know my grandmother is one of the **smartest rodents** I know. She gives the best advice. Like '**Never talk to strangers**' and '**Don't take any wooden nickels**' and

Monster

Mummy

Martian

ampire   Werewolf   Elf   Frankenstein

'**If you're happy and you know it, clap your paws**.' Well, that last one is actually the title of a song she used to sing, but you get the idea. My grandmother's amazing."

He kissed the photo of his **grandmother** that he kept in his wallet.

Then he looked around the room. "Speaking of amazing, Geronimo," he squeaked. "When are you going to set me up with that amazing sister of yours?"

I sighed. All of my friends love my sister, THEA. She is smart, beautiful, and super adventurous. The thing is, my sister has **so many** boyfriends, she can't keep them all straight.

Still, I felt bad for **Hercule**, so I told him I'd see what I could do.

"**Great!**" Hercule shouted happily. "How can I repay you? I know! I'll set you up with my cousin **Brutella Poirat**. You'll love her!"

Brutella Poirat

WHAT'S SQUEAKING?

Before I could **STOP** him, **Hercule** pulled out his cell phone and called his cousin.

"Brutella, what's squeaking? It's your cousin Hercule," he began. "Listen, I want you to meet my friend Geronimo Stilton. You're gonna *love* him. He's not **brave** or **athletic**. In fact, I guess you could say he's an uncoordinated scaredy mouse. That's why I thought of you. You could whip him into shape. Maybe take him to your **WEIGHT-LIFTING CLASS** or show him your karate moves. You're a **BLACK BELT**, right? You two would be great together! Just don't break his tailbone like you did to your last boyfriend."

I chewed my whiskers. Weight lifting?

DISCUS THROWING

FOOTBALL

WEIGHT LIFTING

KARATE

KARATE? Broken TAILBONE? Oh, how did I get myself into these situations?

I started to tell Hercule that I planned on being busy for the next ten million years, but he ignored me.

"It's all set, Geronimo. You call THEA and we'll all go out tomorrow night. This is perfect! Just think of it. If I married your sister . . . and you married my cousin . . . we would be RELATED! Wouldn't that be INCREDIBLE?!" he squeaked happily.

I gulped. It would be incredible, all right. An incredible nightmare! Still, what could I say? Hercule was so EXCITED he looked like he was about to explode. So I plastered a smile on my snout and just nodded. After all, I didn't want to make a scene in the middle of my Halloween party.

Later that night, I **COLLAPSED** into bed and **FELL ASLEEP** instantly. Can you guess what I dreamed about? I'll tell you. I dreamed about **Chuckles** and stolen **pumpkins** and one CRAZY HALLOWEEN I will never forget!

Geronimo

Thea

Hercule

Brutella

A Super-Duper

HALLOWEEN

Party

Note: Before you start organizing a party, ask an adult for help.

Remember that knives and sharp scissors can be dangerous!

SCARY GHOST!

1. Take a balloon, inflate it, and tie it with a long string.

2. In the center of a sheet of tissue paper large enough to cover the balloon, cut a small hole for the string. Be sure to use safety scissors!

3. Insert the balloon's string through the opening.

4. With a black felt-tip pen, draw the ghost's eyes and mouth. Hang it as a decoration.

BAT NAPKIN HOLDER

1. Draw a bat on a piece of construction paper. (See drawing.)

2. Cut along its edges, and then cut an opening along the mouth. (Be sure to use safety scissors.)

3. Wrap the construction paper bat around a rolled napkin and insert its long tail through its mouth.

SCARY FACES!

1. Fold a white, black, or orange sheet of construction paper into an accordion as shown.

2. On the front of the first fold, draw a ghost (A), a bat (B), or a pumpkin (C).

A

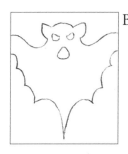

B

C

3. Cut along the edge of the drawing with safety scissors. Then open the paper chain. With a black felt-tip pen, color some scary expressions on every face.

TARANTULA DECORATION

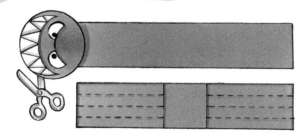

1. Copy the above designs on a sheet of black construction paper. Using safety scissors, cut along the edges of both designs, and cut along the dotted lines.

2. Glue the body to its legs as shown.

3. Roll the body and stick it under its head.

4. To make the tarantula look more realistic, make folds on every leg.

AWESOME STRAWS

1. Make lots of awesome straws for your guests. Draw, color, and cut out black cats, bats, skulls, and spiders from different colored construction paper (always using safety scissors).

2. Put a piece of tape behind each design and attach it to a straw.

WINGED BOTTLES

1. On a sheet of black construction paper, draw wings as shown. Cut them out with safety scissors and attach them with adhesive tape on two sides of a bottle.

2. Draw eyebrows, cut them out, and glue them on the bottle.

3. Draw two circles, cut them out, and color them yellow. Transform them into eyes by coloring the pupils with a black felt-tip pen. Glue them under the eyebrows.

4. Draw a mouth with four teeth, cut it out, and glue it on the bottle as shown.

CONCOCTIONS AND POTIONS

Vampire Juice: Put some ice cubes in a pitcher and fill it with your favorite red punch.

Bug Juice: Fill a pitcher with yellow lemonade. Add a drop of green food coloring.

Bat Juice: Put some ice cubes in a pitcher and fill it with grape juice.

Label each beverage.

MONSTROUS PIZZA

Ingredients: Ready-made pizza crust, tomato sauce, shredded mozzarella, a hard-boiled egg, olives, pineapple slices, small tomato, pepperoni slices.

1. Ask an adult to turn on the oven to 375°F.

2. Spread tomato sauce evenly over pizza crust and sprinkle shredded mozzarella over sauce.

3. Place two half slices of the hard-boiled egg where the eyes should be. Place an olive on the slices to form the pupils.

4. Cut two slices of pineapple into the shape of eyebrows. Place them over eyes as shown.

5. For a nose, put a slice of tomato in the center of the pizza. Use the small slices of pineapple for teeth.

6. Place the pepperoni slices around the face.

7. Bake for about 25 minutes, or follow baking directions on the crust package.

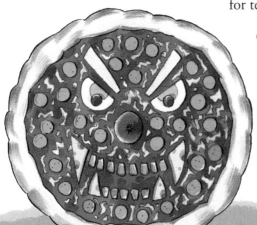

FANCY SANDWICHES

Sarcophagus Feet

1. Take several slices of soft bread and, with the help of an adult, cut them into the shape of feet.

2. On one side, spread some grape jelly. Place grapes on the toes.

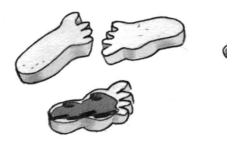

Mummy Dentures

1. Take some slices of soft bread and, with the help of an adult, cut them into the shape of a half moon.

2. Spread cream cheese on one side, then put some pistachio nuts all around the edges.

3. Place another slice of bread on top.

Have a fun and

happy Halloween!

Want to read my next adventure?
I can't wait to tell you all about it!

I'M NOT A SUPERMOUSE!

Yes, it's true—I'm a total 'fraidy mouse and the biggest worryrat. In fact, I'm the complete opposite of my super-sporty and very brave friend Bruce Hyena. That's why I couldn't believe it when he dragged me off on a series of outrageous adventures to toughen me up. I had to keep reminding him that I'm not a supermouse! Or am I?

And don't miss any of my other fabumouse adventures!

#1 LOST TREASURE OF THE EMERALD EYE

#2 THE CURSE OF THE CHEESE PYRAMID

AND MOUSE HAUNTED HOUSE

#4 I'M TOO FOND OF MY FUR!

#5 FOUR MICE DEEP IN THE JUNGLE

#6 PAWS OFF, CHEDDARFACE!

PIZZAS FOR UE COUNT

#8 ATTACK OF THE BANDIT CATS

#9 A FABUMOUSE VACATION FOR GERONIMO

#10 ALL BECAUSE OF A CUP OF COFFEE

HALLOWEEN, 'FRAIDY OUSE!

#12 MERRY CHRISTMAS, GERONIMO!

#13 THE PHANTOM OF THE SUBWAY

#14 THE TEMPLE OF THE RUBY OF FIRE

#15 THE MONA MOUSA CODE

#16 A CHEESE-COLORED CAMPER

#17 WATCH YOUR WHISKERS, STILTON!

#18 SHIPWRE THE PIRATE IS

#19 MY NAME IS STILTON, GERONIMO STILTON

#20 SURF'S UP, GERONIMO!

#21 THE WILD, WILD WEST

#22 THE SE OF CACKLE CASTLE

A CHRISTMAS TALE

#23 VALENTINE'S DAY DISASTER

#24 FIELD TRIP TO NIAGARA FALLS

#25 THE SE FOR SUN TREASU

#26 THE MUMMY WITH NO NAME

#27 THE CHRISTMAS TOY FACTORY

#28 WEDDING CRASHER

#29 DOWN A DOWN UN

**THE MOUSE
ISLAND MARATHON**

**#31 THE MYSTERIOUS
CHEESE THIEF**

**CHRISTMAS
CATASTROPHE**

**#32 VALLEY OF THE
GIANT SKELETONS**

**GERONIMO AND
THE GOLD
MEDAL MYSTERY**

**#34 GERONIMO
STILTON, SECRET
AGENT**

**#35 A VERY
MERRY CHRISTMAS**

**#36 GERONIMO'S
VALENTINE**

**THE RACE
ACROSS AMERICA**

**#38 A FABUMOUSE
SCHOOL
ADVENTURE**

**#39 SINGING
SENSATION**

**#40 THE KARATE
MOUSE**

**MIGHTY MOUNT
KILIMANJARO**

**#42 THE PECULIAR
PUMPKIN THIEF**

*And don't
forget to
look for*

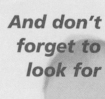

**#43 I'M NOT A
SUPERMOUSE!**

If you like my brother's books, check out the next adventure of the Thea Sisters!

THEA STILTON AND THE MYSTERY IN PARIS

When Colette invites her friends to come home with her to Paris for spring break, the five mice are delighted. While they're in France, they'll even get to attend Colette's fashion-designer friend Julie's runway show at the Eiffel Tower! But soon after the Thea Sisters arrive, Julie's designs are stolen. Will the five mice be able to catch the thief in time to save the fashion show?

Be sure to check out these other exciting Thea Sisters adventures:

**THEA STILTON
AND THE
DRAGON'S CODE**

**THEA STILTON
AND THE
MOUNTAIN OF FIRE**

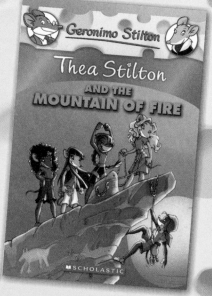

THEA STILTON AND THE GHOST OF THE SHIPWRECK

THEA STILTON AND THE SECRET CITY

ABOUT THE AUTHOR

Born in New Mouse City, Mouse Island, **GERONIMO STILTON** is Rattus Emeritus of Mousomorphic Literature and of Neo-Ratonic Comparative Philosophy. For the past twenty years, he has been running *The Rodent's Gazette,* New Mouse City's most widely read daily newspaper.

Stilton was awarded the Ratitzer Prize for his scoops on *The Curse of the Cheese Pyramid* and *The Search for Sunken Treasure.* He has also received the Andersen 2000 Prize for Personality of the Year. One of his bestsellers won the 2002 eBook Award for world's best ratlings' electronic book. His works have been published all over the globe.

In his spare time, Mr. Stilton collects antique cheese rinds and plays golf. But what he most enjoys is telling stories to his nephew Benjamin.

THE RODENT'S GAZETTE

1. Main entrance
2. Printing presses (where the books and newspaper are printed)
3. Accounts department
4. Editorial room (where the editors, illustrators, and designers work)
5. Geronimo Stilton's office
6. Storage space for Geronimo's books

Map of New Mouse City

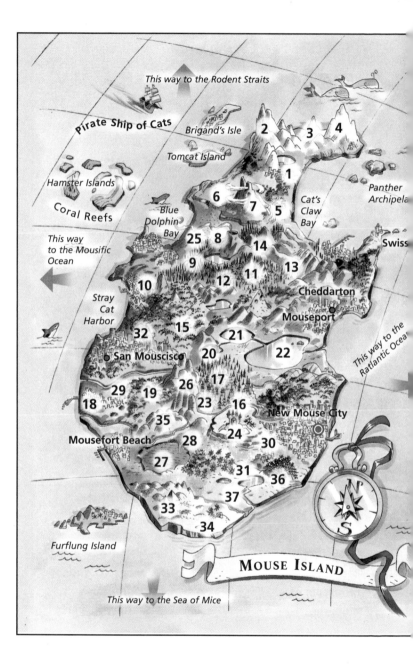

This way to the Rodent Straits

Pirate Ship of Cats

Brigand's Isle

Tomcat Island

2 3 4

1

Hamster Islands

Coral Reefs

Blue Dolphin Bay

6 7 5

Cat's Claw Bay

Panther Archipela

This way to the Mousific Ocean

25 8

14

Swiss

9

13

Cheddarton

Stray Cat Harbor

10

12 11

Mouseport

32 15

21

22

This way to the Ratlantic Ocea

San Mouscisco

20

26 17

29 19

23 16

New Mouse City

18

35

24 30

Mousefort Beach

28

31 36

27

37

33

34

Furflung Island

MOUSE ISLAND

This way to the Sea of Mice

Map of Mouse Island

Dear mouse friends,
Thanks for reading, and farewell
till the next book.
It'll be another whisker-licking-good
adventure, and that's a promise!

Geronimo Stilton